FUG AND

3/18

THE THUMPS

T

FUG AND THE THUMPS

Malachy Doyle

Firefly

First published in 2018
by Firefly Press
25 Gabalfa Road, Llandaff North, Cardiff, CF14 2JJ
www.fireflypress.co.uk

Text copyright © Malachy Doyle

A CIP catalogue record of this book is
available from the British Library.

ISBN 9781910080689
ebook ISBN 9781910080696

This book has been published with the support of
the Welsh Books Council.

Typeset by Elaine Sharples

Printed and bound by Pulsio

for Kay and Conor – stay safe!

1

Runaway

It's 5.30 a.m. I creep downstairs. I feel around in the dark till I find my dad's jacket. I pull his wallet from the inside pocket. Then I take all the notes and go.

It's 6.30. I'm on the first train to the coast. I get off at a tiny village. I find the only shop that's open, and buy some food. Then I follow a footpath out of town.

As I climb down to a beach, I see a kayak, hidden in the dunes. I turn it over and there's a paddle inside.

As soon as I find it, I know what I'm going to do – I'm going to disappear. Off the face of the map. Off the edge of the known world. Because that's all that matters right now. Getting the hell out of here.

There's no life jacket. I know you're supposed to wear one – it's one of the few things I do know about the sea. But it's flat calm out there. There's hardly a ripple.

I drag the thing to the edge of the water and climb in. Then I push off and I'm away. Free at last!

Because I'm on the run from Fug and the Thumps. From Fug and the *freaking* Thumps.

There was no other way to escape them, see. Not at school. Not on the way to school either. The only way to beat them, I soon found out, was to join them. But the only way to join them was to…

Well, I couldn't do it. I wouldn't do it.

I knew what that meant, though. I knew what would happen today and every day, as soon as I set foot on the bus. The same as before, only worse. Much worse, because I'd tried to stand up to them.

So I'd no choice. Really, no choice but to get up in the night, to nick eighty-five quid from my dad and go.

Which is how I ended up here, about fifty miles away, heading out to sea. Because who's going to find you in the deep dark ocean?

And don't tell me that doesn't make any sense, because I don't care any more! I need to get away, right?

Cos they're doing my head in. Fug and the Thumps. They're doing my flipping head in!

I've never done this before, to tell you the truth – this kayaking thing. But I've seen people do it and it always looked pretty easy. Just stick a paddle in the water and off you go.

It's hard to keep the thing straight, though. Especially when the waves keep wanting to send you back where you came from.

I'm thinking maybe I only ever saw it done on a

lake before. It's a whole different ballgame out here on the open sea. With all this wind. All these waves. Not that they're big, but…

When you push the paddle down on one side, the waves turn you sideways before you can get yourself straight by switching it to the other side. And then, because you're sideways to the sea and it's crashing into you, the whole thing starts rocking and water splashes in.

After a while I get a bit of a rhythm going. Left, right. Left, right. More on the left, every now and again, to get the stupid thing facing back out to the ocean. I'm going straight now, most of the time, rather than round and round like a one-legged turtle.

My bum's a bit wet, mind you. There's a load of water sloshing about in the bottom of the kayak. It seems a lot just from the splashing. It's not leaking, is it?

Is there a plug somewhere I pull to let it back out? But wouldn't that just let more in? I don't know. I just hope the damn thing doesn't fill up.

And you're supposed to have some sort of a cover on it, aren't you? To pull up tight round your legs and stop the waves coming in over the top?

It was flat calm when I started, but it's getting a bit rougher now, the further out I go. I twist around to see how far from shore I've got. It's a heck of a long way! Could I make it all the way back if I needed to? Against the tide?

Cos I'm beginning to have second thoughts about this 'needing some space' thing. I mean, the whole damn boat's filling with water!

2

The Island

And then, up ahead, I see it! The island! I knew it was out here somewhere, I just wasn't sure how far.

I head towards it, but the current seems to want to pull me out and round, rather than into shore. It's my only chance, though. I've got to make it happen.

There's a sort of a slipway, so I paddle straight up and onto it. Phew!

But when I try and get out of the boat, my foot skids on the seaweed. I fall forward and whack my head on the side of the kayak.

Slipway? You're damn right, it's a *slip*way! I'm slipping and sliding all over the place, trying to drag the stupid thing up out of the water. I can't even stand, so I end up having to edge round behind it, sit on my bum and try pushing it with my feet.

It's heavy, though, especially with all that water in. And every time I try to push it, all I end up doing is skidding back down the slipway on all that slimy green stuff and then having no end of trouble getting back up to the boat.

I manage to nudge it up a bit and then leave it, crawling up past the seaweed. Who cares? I've reached dry land.

I'm knackered from all that paddling. My arms ache. My back and bum ache. I've a massive great lump the size of an egg on my forehead from when I fell. I'm soaked through. And to top it all, my rucksack, with all the food and stuff, is soaking too. I'd pushed it in down behind the seat, to keep it safe, and forgotten all about it. Even when all the water started coming in. What a thicko!

I check the inside pocket of my coat. At least the money's safe and dry.

There's nothing here. I've been all over the island and there's not a single sign of life. I came across five old cottages, all empty. All falling down.

I saw two done-up ones, but there's nobody living in either of them, that's for sure. They're holiday cottages, I suppose.

Weird place for a holiday, if you ask me. I mean, what are you going to do all day? Stare at the empty sea?

I climb to the highest point of the island, looking back to where I came from. Over there, way in the distance, it's all going on like it always does. Life. School. Fug and the flipping Thumps.

I sit on a rock and eat my soggy sandwich. I chew my soggy crisps. And then I realise how thirsty I am. Why didn't I buy a drink in that stupid shop before I set off? There's water all around me. But not a drop to drink.

I head back to the boat then, to decide what to do next.

But when I get to the slipway, it's gone! The freaking kayak's gone!

I look all around, in case I'm in the wrong place. In case someone somewhere is playing tricks on me.

And then I notice the seaweed's gone too. The water's come up and covered it all. It's nearly reached the top of the slipway.

Oh my god! The tide's come in! It's taken my flipping kayak! Why didn't I pull it up further? What a dimwit!

I look out to sea. There's no sign of it. And then I spot the paddle, way off in the distance, floating. And I won't tell you what I said right then, but I said it VERY VERY LOUD!

So I'm stuck here. On a desert island (except it's not exactly a desert, but you know what I mean). With no food, no drink. Nowhere to get in out of the cold and rain. And no way to get off.

At least there's no sign of Fug and the Thumps. But well done, Ben Hastings. You've really gone and done it now.

3

Break-in

I remember my phone. But it's in my bag, isn't it? Is it wet? Is it ruined?

I wipe it on my shirt and switch it on. It powers up! I ring Mum. But there's no signal.

I trudge back to the top of the hill. If it doesn't work here, it won't work anywhere.

It doesn't connect.

So what do I do now? I could try and swim

back to the mainland, but it's way too far. I've never been much of a swimmer really.

I could stand on a rock and wave down a passing boat. But I haven't seen a single one all day.

I could light a fire, maybe, and hope someone spots it. But the rain's coming in. The sky's darkening.

I'm going to have to get into one of the holiday houses. I try all the doors, then all the windows.

'What's the point?' I yell. What's the point in locking a place when there's nobody here? I mean, it's not exactly the sort of area where a gang of teenage hoodlums are going to break in and trash the joint!

I could try and find some cover in one of the tumble-downs, I suppose. I'm cold and wet. I need food and water. I need to find a phone that works, to let my folks know I'm OK. And if no one can come and get me tonight, I need a bed.

So there's nothing else for it – I chuck a stone at one of the windows, pull away the broken glass and climb through.

I go to put on the lights but I can't find a switch. I go all round the walls before I realise why.

There's no electricity! What sort of back-of-beyond place is this? I thought everywhere had flipping electricity these days!

I spot a torch, hanging on a nail. Phew – the battery still works. I rummage around in the drawers till I find some matches and light a few candles. I even manage to get an oil lamp going. Clever kid!

I look around. There's no phone. I check the drawers – no mobiles. (Not that they'd work anyway.)

I run the tap. At least there's water – though it's probably just stuff that's been trickling down the roof, from the look of the giant tank outside. I'm not sure how safe it is – those tiles don't look like they've been cleaned in a long time – but I take a long cold drink. Beggars can't be choosers. I hope I don't poison myself, though – that's the last thing I need.

Running away sure puts a hunger on you. Never mind paddling for hours (well, it felt like hours). So I look for the fridge. Oh yeah, no fridge. Luckily there's a load of tins in the cupboard. I grab some beans, manage to light the gas and, wow, they don't half taste good!

Now I've got all that sorted, it's time to look at the real problem. How am I going to get off this stupid island? Because it's all right for a night, maybe, but I can't stay here forever. Mum and Dad will be up the wall already. Specially Dad, when he checks his wallet.

And here I am, miles away on a deserted island. With no way of getting off. No way of even getting a message to anyone.

Because yeah, I've got away from Fug and the damn Thumps. Which is good. You can't imagine how good.

But you know what they say about out of the frying pan…?

4

Thump in the Night

Well, there's nothing I can do about it now, in the dark. So sleep on it, kid. Maybe things won't seem so bad in the morning.

I try the most comfortable-looking bed. But it's like in Goldilocks – it's way too big, and just reminds me how alone I am here.

I try one of the bunk beds in the other room, but I can't seem to sleep there either. In the end I drag a duvet through to the sofa and curl up on that.

At least that way I can keep an eye on the front door. I know there's no one outside, of course, but it's so flipping dark out there. And when you break into a house, you just can't seem to settle. You think some mad axeman owner's going to turn up at any moment, seeking revenge.

It's weird, actually. I don't want anyone to come, because I know I'll get the biggest telling-off in my life. For skipping school. For nicking a load of money off my dad. For not telling my folks where I'm going. And then – horror of horrors – staying out overnight.

For pinching a kayak, too. For risking my neck in the open sea – without a life jacket. For losing the stupid kayak. For breaking into someone's house. For scoffing all their beans...

But if anyone does come, I want to make sure they find me. Because how else am I going to get out of this place?

Unless it's Fug, of course. He's the one person I do *not* want to find me.

I can't seem to escape from him, though. I can't get him out of my brain, even when I do finally sleep. There he is, the boy of my dreams, standing at the end of the bed with that sick-looking smirk on his face. Watching his gang lay into me.

Not Fug, though. He never lays a finger on anyone. He doesn't have to.

'Get them off me!' I'm yelling, as I wake. My head's throbbing. My back and arms are aching.

And then I remember whacking my skull on the side of the kayak. And the effort of paddling across an open sea.

I eventually fall asleep again, but this time it's more like remembering than dreaming. Remembering my first day at school. There he was, Fug, demanding my dinner money. And what did I do? I gave it to him.

Day after day. Week after week. If I'd already given it to Miss and didn't have any for him, he'd set the Thumps on me. At break. Behind the bike shed.

They said if I yelled, they'd hit me even harder. And if I told anyone … they'd kill me.

I took to raiding my mum's purse before

school. Sliding up to Fug on the bus and handing him enough to keep him happy. To keep the heavy squad off me.

And so it went on, month after month. Till the other day.

'You want us to stop, kid? You want us to pick on someone else for a change?'

I knew I wasn't the only one. I'm not stupid. But I nodded. There was nothing I wanted more.

'OK,' said Fug, looking me right between the eyes. 'From now on you're one of us – a Thump.' And he raised his palm, to high-five me.

But I turned and walked away.

5

Drowning

In the morning, I'm more tired than when I went to bed. Nightmares can do that to you.

I check every window. There's no sign of anyone. I go down to the shore. There are no boats. I go back and warm up another can of beans. You could get bored of beans.

Then I walk the island again, looking for a way to get off.

At last, at long last, I see a boat off in the distance. It's a fisherman, checking his pots, by the look of it. I wave. I shout. I jump up and down and scream. But he never once looks my way. Never hears me, over the sound of his engine. And then he's gone, damn it!

I keep walking, keep looking. And then I spot it! The kayak! It washed up back on the far side of the island! My luck's turning, huh?

It's wedged between some rocks. There's a great gash down one side, but I can't see any water inside, so I suppose it's OK.

I drag it off the rocks. I check to see if there's any more damage. A few bumps and bashes, but nothing too bad by the look of it. Now all I need is a paddle.

Before I go looking, I remember about the tide. So I haul the thing up onto the grass, well past the seaweed line. High tide line, that's what it's called. See, I'm not a complete twit.

I don't know if the water level's going up or down, mind you – how are you supposed to tell? But I'm not taking any risks. Not this time.

So where am I going to find a paddle? I go back to the slipway and look around. There's a knackered old rowing boat. All rotten and full of holes. No way that's going anywhere!

There's a hut. I can't get inside. Outside, round the back, I find an oar. One oar. It's got a nasty-looking crack in it, and I know it's meant for a rowing boat, but it's my best bet.

I grab it and head for the kayak. I launch myself into the water and start paddling.

It's useless. The oar's too big, too heavy. I'm trying to swap sides every stroke, like you're supposed to. But by the time I get the great lumbering thing back in, the tide's spun me round.

The current's pulling me out into deep water – which is what I wanted, I suppose. But there's no way I can control it. And the kayak's filling up with water, way faster than it did before. If I don't do something quick, I'm in real trouble.

I let go of the stupid oar. It's useless anyway. I try to paddle with my hands, back to shore. But the sea's too strong. The boat's too heavy. The current's pulling me out, always out, into deeper and deeper water.

And the waves. They're really bad on this side of the island. I suppose it's not sheltered, like it was before. It's the open sea here. The wide open ocean, with bigger winds, bigger waves…

There's only one thing to do. I've no choice. I wriggle up, get my legs out, and tip myself over the side.

Deep down, under the water. Under the water, deep down.

And then I'm on the surface again, gasping for breath. Somehow the kayak's still there, next to me. I grab hold of it, sucking in air. But blimey, the water's *freezing*!

I edge round to the back of the kayak and kick out, trying to push the thing back to shore. If I hang onto it, I'll stay afloat. If I get it back to the island I can try again. Find a better paddle…

But no. It's not going to work. The current's too strong – it's taking us further and further out. The island's slipping away. I don't know if I can swim that far.

Again, I've no choice. I push off from the boat and start swimming. But the current's crazy. With every pull I make back towards the island, I can feel the tide fighting me. Forcing me further from the shore.

It's me against the full force of the sea. I fight it. I fight it. I swim. I swim.

After a while I'm not even sure where I am any more. What direction I'm going in, forward or back. I'm losing confidence. Losing strength.

But while I still have power in my arms, power in my legs, I keep going. There's no alternative.

Well, there is one alternative. But I'm not going there. I've too much to live for…

My knee! I've just whacked it on some freaking great rock!

And then I realise, hey! That means I've made it to shore! I've done it!

I'm clean out of breath, though. I've swallowed a load of water, the gravel's sliding away under me, and the waves are sucking me back in.

I slip and go under. I drag myself up. My knees rip on the stones. I thump into another rock. But I will not give up. I am the one and only Ben Hastings, and I will NEVER give up!

I haul myself up on the shore, retching, gasping for breath. I've lost the oar. I've lost the stupid kayak again. I'm half dead, three-quarters frozen. But at least I'm alive.

6

Who cares?

Back to the holiday house. I borrow some clothes.
I look like a tramp, but who the hell cares?

More beans. I'm farting like a trooper. But who
cares about that either?

I wonder what's going on out there in the real
world. There's no TV here, so I can't tell if I'm on
the news yet. I probably am. I mean, when kids go
missing they're always on the news, aren't they?

They have search parties. Everybody in the whole neighbourhood goes out looking for them.

The trouble is, I'm more than fifty miles from home. Nobody's got a clue where I am. The chances of someone coming across me, just by chance, are next to nothing. Summer's over. The holiday-homes people are gone, back to real life. And nobody else sets foot on this place, not even that lonesome fisherman, by the look of it.

I suppose the shop woman, in the village where I got off the train, might remember me. But she was a doddery old thing, half way to the grave. I don't think she even looked up at me.

Someone on the train maybe? Or the guy at the station? But even if they do remember me, I don't see how they're going to track me down to here. It's the last place in the world anyone's likely to look.

It's up to me then. Ben Hastings. Either I find some way to get off this stupid island, or a way to let people know I'm here.

Because, yeah, I'd no choice. I had to get away from Fug and his Thumps. But now that I'm here, in the one place they're never going to find me, I'm not so sure how clever it was.

Maybe I should have done what they wanted? It wouldn't have been so hard, would it? Just put pressure on a few of the younger ones. Twist a few arms, while nobody's looking (none of the teachers, that is). Thump any that don't come up with the goods, any that don't do what you tell them. Put the fear of god into any of the braver ones – the sort that might tell.

Happens everywhere. It's just a part of growing up, isn't it? A way of learning where you fit in, how you fit in? Just a way of learning to respect your elders and betters.

Except it isn't. It's not growing up. It's not learning. And I couldn't do it. It's not who I am. It's not part of a world I want to live in.

The fear on their faces when they'd see Fug looking at them. I can remember it, clear as day. And then, when he'd point at them, they'd be wetting themselves. That or running. Into the welcoming arms of the Thumps.

Maybe I should have stood up to them, good and proper. Maybe running away like I did was only that – running away. Running scared. Yet again. Yellow-bellied Hastings.

I force open the door of the hut by the slipway. There are old broken lobster pots, rubbish, bits of old engine. Nothing useful.

I search all round the house I'm staying in. I find a radio, but the batteries are dead. In a shed, out the back, there's a bucket and spade. Maybe I could dig my way home?

Up in the rafters, I spot a surfboard. No way, kid – don't even think of it.

There's a fishing rod, though. It might come in handy if I run out of beans. Not that I know how to fish. If I did manage to catch anything, I'd have to kill it, and I can't even hit people, never mind killing things.

I go over to the other holiday house. There's nothing much outside. Nothing useful anyway. I think I'm going to have to break in here too. Blimey, I'm turning into a right bad 'un. Fug'd be proud of me.

I lob a rock through one of the windows. I try not to rip my arm open as I clamber through, stepping over the broken glass.

I check the food stocks. Enough to keep me going for a few more days, if I need it.

Then I spot a tiny radio. No batteries, but there's some sort of a handle. I pull it out, shake the thing, and hear a bit of music.

Aha! A wind-up radio! I spin it, giving it all I've got, and it takes me right through the next song and into the news…

'Police are on the look-out for Ben Hastings, a twelve-year-old boy who disappeared from…'

The charge runs out. Wind it, kid! Wind it!

'Search parties are combing the area where he lives. The public are asked to get in touch if they have any information…'

Search parties! I was hoping there'd be search parties. Wind it! Wind it!

And then I hear Mum! It's my mum!

'Please come back, Ben, love. Nobody's cross with you. We just want you home, safe and well.'

Then Dad. *'And please, if anyone knows where he is… If anyone's got him,'* he says, voice cracking, *'we beg you…'*

He's crying. It's Dad and Mum, on the radio, crying.

7

S.O.S.

I go down to the slipway and wait for the fishing boat to come past again.

I don't care how long it takes. I'll shout. I'll whistle. I'll fart and set light to it to make a flare... Whatever it takes to get someone's attention.

I wait all day and there's no sign of him. No sign of anyone. Why doesn't the stupid fisherman come back? Doesn't he have to check his pots? Isn't he supposed to do it every day?

The only sign of life is a seal, popping his head up to see who I am. Coming in closer when I call to him. Well, who else is there to talk to?

'How are you doing, seal? Is it cold out there? Did you catch any fish today? Have you seen that fisherman? If you do, tell him to come and get me, will you? I'm getting a bit fed up out here, to tell you the truth. It's not exactly the most exciting holiday destination in the universe, is it? Not exactly Disneyland. Not exactly the Costa del Sol.'

I go back inside. It must be about time for the local news. I wind up the radio again and it's already started...

'One of his friends, Francis Green, is with me, here at the school gates. Anything you'd like to say, Francis?'

Oh my god. Fug. Pretending to be my best buddy.

'Yeah, we're all really worried about him. Ben's a good mate and he'd do anything you ask, pretty much. All we want is for him to come back. We just want to tell him how much we care about him.'

I nearly spew. Francis Ultan Green (Fug for short) always was a good liar, but this is the worst yet. It makes me sick, how he can twist adults round his little finger. How no one sees what he's up to. Not the teachers, not the head…

I mean, no twelve-year-old boy's going to say, 'We just want to tell him how much we care.' Anyone with an ounce of sense can tell he's lying through his stinking teeth!

But adults – they can be so dense sometimes. They just hear what they want to hear. They just want an easy life, that's what I think. I mean, would they even believe me if I told them what Fug's been doing for years? What he's been making other people do?

And if Fug found out that anyone had squealed on him – well, life wouldn't be worth living.

The reporter asks him another question.

'Have you any idea why Ben might have run away, Francis? Was there anything going on in school that he might have been upset about?'

'Upset?' He thinks he's being challenged, and if there's one thing Fug can't stand, it's being challenged. *'Why would he be upset?'*

'Oh, I don't know. Exams. Bullying. That sort of thing,' says the reporter. She's just floundering around, filling up time. Hasn't a clue who she's talking to. But Fug sounds worried.

'*Why are you asking me?*' he says. And I can hear the anger in his voice. He's fighting it, I know – trying to stop it showing on national radio – but there's nothing Fug can do once he lets the anger in. Nothing but explode. Or get someone to do his dirty work for him.

'*How would I know?*' he says, all sneery-like. '*I hardly even knew him…*'

'*But you just said he was a good mate.*'

'*Did I? Well, yeah. Everyone's friends in our school, aren't they? But I don't know him. Not really…*' He's well and truly rattled. Trying too hard to get off the hook, before he's even on it. And I don't know if the reporter can tell yet. But I can.

He's gone too far this time, that's the thing. Gone too far and and he knows it. He's picked the wrong person to try and break. Me. Ben Hastings.

And because of what he's done to me, because of what I've done in response, the whole world's going to find out. About his cruelty, his bullying.

So what I can really hear in Fug's voice is fear. Fear that he'll be found out for who he is, at last.

And the power's shifting. From him. To me. It's shifting.

8

Whoosh, Bang!

I go out, after dark, and flash the torch. What is it you're meant to do? Dot dot dot, dash, dash dash, dot dot dot...

I worry about the battery running out and not finding any more. But hell – I've got to get off this stupid island. I've got to get back there and tell the truth for once. See if I can get someone to believe me. Someone who can actually do something about it.

I find a proper whistle at the back of a kitchen drawer, run out and blow it. Hard and long. Over and over. Three times, isn't it? Three long blasts, then a silence.

But the wind's getting up. The sea's getting rougher. The rain's come in, so I go back inside. And by morning I can't even see the mainland any more.

I find a load of stones and spell out HELP on the beach. Above the high tide line, of course.

But the sea's bigger. The weather's turned. High tide, when it does come, is even higher than before. It wipes out my message. So I have to do it all over again. Only this time I write SOS, because it's quicker.

I tear up a sheet and write SOS on that too, in really big letters. Then I tie it to a length of wood and struggle up the hill.

Blimey, the wind's pretty strong up here! Anyway, I wedge the wood in the rocks at the top, leaving the sheet blowing like a flag. Maybe someone might see it from the mainland. Someone with binoculars. Or someone flying overhead. My own personal search party. If anyone's still looking.

I've run out of baked beans. I'm on to tins of tuna. The gas for the cooker ran out in the first house, so I'm over in the other one now. The one where I found the wind-up radio. I give it a quick twirl…

'Search parties are being scaled down in the hunt for missing schoolboy Ben Hastings. After four days, with no news, the police say that hope is fading…'

Four days! Is that all they're going to give me? That poor kid in the south of France – aren't they still looking for her after ten years or so?

I'd a terrible night, last night. No sleep at all. I just lay there, tossing and turning and listening to the wind and rain. But I've decided what to do. It's down to me now.

They've given up on me already. They couldn't care less if I live or die. (Except Mum and Dad. They always care.) But four measly days! Is that all I'm worth?

It's not as if anybody's going to stumble across me by chance. There's nobody coming out to the island. No boats on the sea because it's so rough. So they're not going to just spot me by accident. I'm going to have to show them where I am. I'm going to have to force them to pay attention.

I spend the day bringing all the rubbish I can find to the old fishing hut by the slipway. Paper, cans, cardboard, broken chairs, old bits of bed, driftwood… Anything really. Anything that'll burn.

I wait till dark and then I stick a lit candle in under it all and stand well back.

Whoosh! Up it goes. The flames are leaping, dancing.

Bang! A can explodes and I run for it.

Whoosh! An even bigger one. Probably the oil can. Or the engine.

Soon the whole hut's going up. The sea lights up all around. Someone's sure to see it. I mean, what about the coastguard? Isn't that their job – looking out to sea for weird stuff going on?

I wait. All night I wait. And no one comes. All the next morning I wait, but still no one comes.

'Come ON!' I yell. 'Don't you even WANT to find me any more? Don't you even CARE! Doesn't anyone even CARE!'

Well, if that didn't work, there's only one thing left to do. Only one way to get the big wide world to notice me.

And it's not a flipping message in a bottle.

9

Arson

This time it'll be bigger. Much bigger. And I'll do it in daylight, when there's more people around to see it. It won't be as bright, I know, but there'll be smoke. Lots of smoke.

Arson. A nasty word for a nasty business. It means burning stuff down. On purpose. Not something you're supposed to do, I know. But I need to get off this island – before I die of hunger, boredom or beans.

The fishing hut wasn't big enough. The flames weren't high enough. It didn't throw up enough smoke. Maybe you couldn't see it from the mainland. Maybe nobody was awake in the middle of the night. Maybe even the coastguard fell asleep.

So this time I'm going to put on a real show. One that the fisherman can't fail to spot. Or the coastguard. Or anyone who's looking out for me (if anyone's bothered any more).

Yes, this time I'll put on a show you could spot from outer space, if you're looking hard enough. This time I'm going to burn down a house.

Sorry, owners – but it's a holiday house. It's not as if you live in it. So yeah, I'm sorry I've got to burn it down. But I've only one life to live, and I want to get on with it.

I know I've got problems right now, back home. But being there is better than being stuck out here on an empty island for the rest of my days. Which won't be many, at this rate.

So I've got to get going. Before the food runs out. Before Mum and Dad give up on me. Before everyone forgets I ever lived.

First I turn on the midday news – and it's all about me again.

'*Ben was the best.*' It's Winkle, the head. I don't know whether I'm pleased, because he sounds as if he actually really rather likes me. Or furious, because he's given up on me already. What do you mean 'was', you stupid old fart? I'm over here. Waving, not drowning.

'*Everyone was fond of him,*' he carries on. '*Ben was a quiet, thoughtful sort of boy with a great future ahead of him. He might not have been the brightest boy in class, but he was always kind to the younger ones…*'

What? I'm dead and you're telling people I'm a thicko! I always thought you were one of the good guys, but I've gone right off you now, mate.

I fling the radio into a corner and go and find the matches. I'll show you, Willie Winkle. I'll show everyone.

It's not raining, for once, so now's the time to do it. I stuff a load of paper into the cushions on the sofa. I pour on the remaining oil from the lamp. I drag all the bedding in and pile that on top. I pull the table and chairs over and lean them against it. Hey, it's going to be quite some bonfire! Then I light a newspaper, toss it at the sofa, and run.

There's a blinding flash of light. I fall.

I stagger to my feet. The room's filling with smoke.

I run towards the door. Where's the door? I trip over something and fall to the floor again.

The door – it's over there. I get back up. But I can't see! *I can't breathe!*

It's better on the floor. There's still some air down there. So I drop down again, and somehow feel my way across the room. But it's hot. It's so hot!

When I reach the doorway, I get to my feet, slam the thing shut behind me, and run.

My clothes are on fire! I'm burning!

10

Come on, you guys!

I run to the rocks. I dive in the sea. Jeez, it's so cold!

I pull myself out of the water, to check I'm OK. Then I turn to look at the damage.

Already the flames have burst through the upstairs windows. There's banging and popping. Stuff's going off like fireworks. Blimey, that was close!

Soon the fire is coming through the roof. Jets of flame, high into the air! Even from here, the heat's incredible.

And then the smoke, that horrible choking smoke starts billowing out and upwards. Smoke from the sofas, the mattresses, the roof timbers… That's what nearly got me, but it's what'll save me, too.

Because people will see it. People just have to see it. As long as it doesn't rain too hard, it'll keep going for ages and ages. They can't possibly miss it, even on the mainland. They can't ignore me this time!

I make my way to the other holiday house, keeping well back from the fire. First thing I do is drink a load of water. I couldn't care less any more whether it's poisoned. I'm dying of thirst anyway.

I check my burns. My hands and face are coming up in blisters. They hurt like hell.

I find some ointment in the bathroom and dab it on. There's a big roll of bandage stuff, so I wrap it round my hands. Gently, like.

Then I get some spare clothes and wrap a scarf round my head, gently as well, to protect myself from the smoke and fumes. I head over to the slipway to wait for the rescue party.

Someone's got to see this! I mean, come on, guys, I know you can't get a fire engine out here, but you're surely not going to let a whole, perfect holiday house burn to the ground, are you? Not without checking out what's going on! I mean, it must be worth a fortune!

And what if there's a real live person out here, have you thought of that? How else could it have gone on fire? I mean, it's not an electrical fault – there isn't any electricity!

So what about that missing kid? The one you've been talking about on the radio all week. You know, Ben Hastings? You haven't forgotten him already, have you?

I'm coughing still. My face and hands are killing me. But it was worth it. Surely it was worth it?

Trouble is, the wind's blowing all the smoke out to sea. Come on, wind, change direction!

I'm terrified the fire'll go out before anyone's spotted it. So I drag a mattress over – the one I've been sleeping on – from the other house. I've got to keep the smoke going.

It's still too hot to go near, of course – I may be stupid, but I'm not that stupid. So I leave the thing outside till I can get a bit closer.

I'm sorry, island. Bit by bit I'm destroying you. But I just want to *live*!

I go for a walk, down by the shore. It is a heck of a lot cooler, away from the flames. I'm looking up, every now and again, for signs of rescue. A helicopter? A giant fire extinguisher?

I'm looking out to sea. A boat? That stupid kayak again?

My friend the seal pops up. I can see the alarm in his eyes, even from here.

'It's all right,' I tell him. 'I won't hurt you. I'm just burning the island.'

But I'm not, am I? Because the island isn't a holiday house or a fishing hut. It's a shame I had to burn them, but what choice did I have? No, the island is the rocks and the beaches. It's the birds and the flowers. The wind and the waves. The sand and the soil. It's the crabs in the rockpools. The rabbits, the hares, the cries of the gulls.

The island will still be around long after I've stopped bothering it – and it'll have one more story to tell.

Just like I'll still be around, long after Fug and the Thumps have stopped bothering me. Well, that's the hope, anyway.

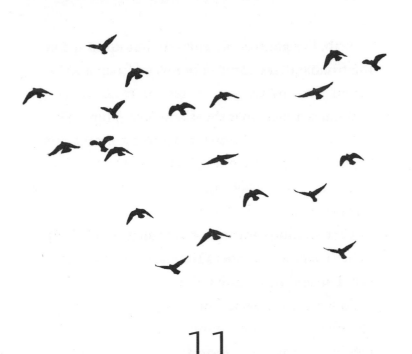

11

The Courage of a Lion

Because yeah, I'm going to be in trouble when I get home. You can't go burning down people's houses – and nearly killing yourself into the bargain – without getting into *big* trouble.

Never mind nicking eighty-five quid off your very own dad. Never mind all the other crazy stuff I've done over the past few days. (I'll be giving him most of the money back, mind you. There's not a lot to spend it on out here.)

Yeah. I've got trouble coming. But nothing like the trouble that's coming the way of Fug and his stupid Thumps. Oh yes.

Because that's what the island's taught me. That I'm strong. That I don't have to be afraid any more. That if I've got a problem, no matter how big, I can find a way to do something about it. I don't have to run away from it.

That 'finding some space' isn't all it's cracked up to be. That there comes a time when you've got to stand up and be counted.

So when I get back, I'm going to do something about Fug and those Thumps. Oh yes. Not just for me. For all the other kids, too. All the ones now, all the ones in the future.

Cos I'm not scared of him any more. Cos, just like the flipping Lion in the flipping *Wizard of Oz*, I've found my courage, because:

1. I refused to do their dirty work. Right at the start of all this, before I even set foot on this stupid island, I put my foot down and said 'No!'
2. I nicked eighty-five smackers from my dad. He'll be *mad* at me!

3. I skipped school. *They'll* be mad at me!
4. I paddled out to sea in a leaky kayak. Without a life jacket. Don't do this at home, kids.
5. I bust into a couple of holiday homes and nicked a load of food.
6. I took off to open sea again, without even a paddle.
7. I bailed out and swam to shore.
8. I blew up a fishing hut, for flip's sake.
9. And then I burnt down a holiday home!

Every one of them, crazy or not, wrong or not, took courage. And if I can do all that, I can go back to the very first one – standing up to Fug – and do it right this time.

Because it's not enough to say no any more. I've got to *stop* him!

So first I'm going to tell my parents everything he's been doing. I'm going to have to anyway, because how else are they going to understand why I did what I did? Why I put them through all this.

Together, me and my folks, we'll tell the teachers. We'll tell the head.

Together, we'll tell the kids in school that it's

going to stop. Everything that's been going on, everything that's been turning them into damaged little worry-monsters, like me… It's all going to really, truly, actually STOP!

That's what'll happen, right?

12

Watch Out, World!

I can hear something…

I can see something…

Here they come! HERE THEY FREAKING COME – THE RESCUE SQUAD!

Now, watch out world – I'm on the way back!

13

Running

I step off the boat and there's Mum, rushing towards me. With tears streaming down her face.

Behind her is Dad, with the biggest smile ever!

And behind him – I can't believe it – there's a load of people with cameras. TV cameras, by the look of it!

And behind them. Half my flipping school! Half the whole damn town!

Mum's hugging me now, like she'll never let me go. But I'm looking over her shoulder. Scanning the crowd.

And there he is. Standing to one side. Francis Ultan Green. With that look in his eye – that cold hard look that can freeze you to the spot. That can make you do anything he damn well wants.

He glances round to check no one's watching him. Fixes me with his eye again, to make sure I don't look away.

He points a finger at me, before pressing it to his lips. Then slowly, ever so slowly, he slides it across his throat.

Only something's different. I can sense, even from here, that Fug's going through the motions. That his heart's not in it.

I narrow my eyes and zoom in on him, just like the camera's zooming in on me…

As the woman with the microphone shoves it in my face, and the very first question comes – 'Why did you do it, Ben?'

I'm not returning her gaze. I'm staring at Fug, straight and hard.

There's a long, long silence – way too long for TV. And the cameras, realising I'm not going to answer, I'm not even going to look at them, turn to follow my gaze. So do the reporters, the teachers, half the flipping school, half the whole damn town…

And I see it on Fug's face. For the first time ever. That look. The look that he could put on his victim, just by giving you the eye, just by pointing a finger at you. That fear that makes your eyes open wide, your body shut down. That makes your knees turn to jelly. That makes you either run, or wet yourself.

Well, I'm the one doing the pointing now. Me and the world's cameras. And Fug's the one with that look on his face, now that everyone's staring at him. It's a look of fear. Pure and absolute fear.

Because he's been found out, at last – and the whole world's watching. The game's up, Francis Ultan Green. Your bullying days are over…

Because me, Ben Hastings, I'm the one that's doing the looking. Yes, I'm the one that's doing the pointing. And it's you, Francis Green, whose knees have turned to jelly. You, Francis Green, whose courage melts to custard.

Because there's you, on one side, full of hate. And on the other there's everyone else, full of joy, to see me safe and well.

So where's your jolly gang of Thumps now, kid? They know which side their bread's buttered on, that's what – and they've switched to the winning team.

Leaving you on your own, with your bitter, twisted nastiness, Francis Green. So who's got the power now, kid? Who's the one with no one looking out for them now, kid?

Suddenly he's running. He's turned and he's running. From me, from the cameras, from the whole damn world…

It's Fug the bully-boy. Running scared.